NEW DIMENSION

Apostle Prof. Johnson Suleman

NEW DIMENSION
Apostle Prof. Johnson Suleman
Copyright@ October 2023

Published in Nigeria by
Hosanna Publishers
Km 132 Benin-Okene/ Abuja Express way,
Auchi, Edo State, Nigeria
Tel: +2348106468478

TABLE OF CONTENT.

The constant desire and aspiration of everyone is to progressively move from one height to another. Having lofty desires are not enough in the emergence of champions. Specifically, the transformation and transfer of Mephibosheth from Lodebar to the king's palace provided useful lessons with which myriad of other adjoining lessons were brought forth. A new dimension is beyond wishes, you possess it. The man who remembers you should be the focus, and not the one who brings your shortcomings to the fore. No act of kindness shown to anyone that will not be reciprocated.

Jonathan loved David with extreme practicalities even when there were enough justifiable, though sentimental reasons to act in the contrary. The seed Jonathan sowed in the life of David was reaped by Mephibosheth. There is no need arguing with the distracter; your sent help can't be diverted. Ziba's response to the question of King David was enough to stop the lifting of Mephibosheth, but the voice of the father's seed was stronger.

In this book, there are practical lessons on how to make your life great and expressive. Nothing may change around you until you place a demand on them. Your infuriation for a change is what you need to cause a permanent turn around.

1.

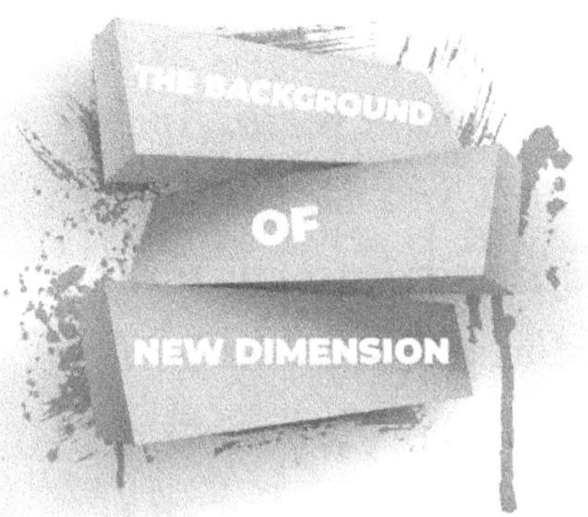

*A*nd David said, Is there yet any that is left of the house of Saul, that I may shew him kindness for Jonathan's sake? And there was of the house of Saul a servant whose name was Ziba. And when they had called him unto David, the king said unto him, Art thou Ziba? And he said, Thy servant is he. And the king said, Is there not yet any of the house of Saul, that I may shew the kindness of God unto him? And Ziba said unto the king, Jonathan hath yet a son, which is lame on his feet. And the king said unto him, Where is he? And Ziba said unto the king, Behold, he is in the house of Machir, the son of Ammiel, in Lodebar. Then

King David sent, and fetched him out of the house of Machir, the son of Ammiel, from Lodebar. Now when Mephibosheth, the son of Jonathan, the son of Saul, was come unto David, he fell on his face, and did reverence. And David said, Mephibosheth. And he answered, Behold thy servant! And David said unto him, Fear not: for I will surely shew thee kindness for Jonathan thy father's sake, and will restore thee all the land of Saul thy father; and thou shalt eat bread at my table continually. And he bowed himself, and said, What is thy servant, that thou shouldest look upon such a dead dog as I am? Then the king called to Ziba, Saul's servant, and said unto him, I have given unto thy master's son all that pertained to Saul and to all his house. Thou therefore, and thy sons, and thy servants, shall till the land for him, and thou shalt bring in the fruits, that thy master's son may have food to eat: but Mephibosheth thy master's son shall eat bread alway at my table. Now Ziba had fifteen sons and twenty servants. Then said Ziba unto the king, According to all that my lord the king hath commanded his servant, so shall thy servant do. As for Mephibosheth, said the king, he shall eat at my table, as one of the king's sons. And Mephibosheth had a young son, whose name was Micha. And all that dwelt in the house of Ziba were servants unto Mephibosheth. So Mephibosheth dwelt in Jerusalem: for he did eat continually at the king's table; and was lame on both his feet. {II Samuel 9:1-13 KJV}

New heights and levels don't come by coincidence, they are triggered. The probabilities of a new dimension are a huge possibility. You don't wish for better life, you possess it. The *"possessing of possession"* is never passive, but active with principles guiding the step-by-step actualization of same just the same way miracles are worked out. New dimensions are deliberately snatched or taken. So, what exactly is a new dimension? The life of Mephibosheth is a definition of the new dimension in this context. In II Samuel 4:4, Mephibosheth became a product of misfortune, which stagnated him on one spot. He was just five years old when he reportedly fell from the back of his nurse. The bad news was not the fall and subsequently becoming incapacitated, but the bereavement that followed. Actually, the news of Mephibosheth losing his father and grandfather on the same day at the same instance was broken to them.

And Jonathan, Saul's son, had a son that was lame of his feet. He was five years old when the tidings came of Saul and Jonathan out of Jezreel, and his nurse took him up, and fled: and it came to pass, as she made haste to flee, tat he fell, and became lame. And his name was Mephibosheth. {II Samuel 4:4 KJV}

His misadventure was beyond double tragedy. He became fatherless and equally lost the royalty on the same day. As he struggled to adapt to the unfortunate condition and circumstance, those who were supposed to take care of him took advantage of him. Mephibosheth's grandfather, Saul, lost his life and the throne in one day. The heir apparent, Jonathan, had equally fallen to cruel hands of death. Matter became worsened for Mephibosheth and his family, because he couldn't even talk about the throne having become lame. Remember, according to II Samuel 5:8, the lame, blind and the leprous were not supposed to appear before the king, let alone being crowned as king. Ziba, the servant of Saul, whose natural duty was to see to the wellbeing of Mephibosheth, relocated him to Lodebar. Lodebar was a place of low pasture, which means opportunities of expression were limited even for the physically fit. If survival was difficult for the physically fit in Lodebar, what about the lame? Therefore, if there is any situation that can be described as hopeless and despondent, Mephibosheth's own was.

I will overturn, overturn, overturn, it: and it shall be no more, until he come whose right it is; and I will give it him. {Ezekiel 21:27 KJV}

There are three basic triggers of a new dimension. They are; (i) reaction (ii) enforcement (iii) information.

(i) Reaction

No condition changes without a reaction. The several actions of Jonathan in I Samuel 19:1-2, I Samuel 20:9-16, I Samuel 20:4 and I Samuel 20:30-34 triggered David's reaction in II Samuel 9:1-13. Every condition remains the same until there is a reaction. Reactions don't just occur, they are triggered. What have you done that can initiate reaction into a new dimension. Mephibosheth benefitted some of the good will of the father, Jonathan. Even though Jonathan knew he was the heir apparent, yet he supported David who was an anointed king in waiting. If all your actions and reactions are based on primordial sentiments, you can't take destiny changing decisions. All decisions must not be predicated on sensory perceptions. There are tangible realities beyond what the optical eyes can see. Jonathan may not have been able to explain his decision, but he sowed worthy seeds ahead of his child.

Then Saul's anger was kindled against Jonathan, and he said unto him, Thou son of the perverse rebellious woman, do not I know that thou hast chosen the son of Jesse to thine own confusion, and unto the confusion of thy mother's nakedness? For as long as the son of Jesse liveth upon the ground, thou shalt not be established, nor thy kingdom. Wherefore now send and fetch him unto me, for he shall surely die. And Jonathan answered Saul his father, and said unto him, Wherefore shall he be slain? what hath he done? And Saul cast a javelin at him to smite him: whereby Jonathan knew that it was determined of his father to slay David. So Jonathan arose from the table in fierce anger, and did eat no meat the second day of the month: for he was grieved for David, because his father had done him shame. {I Samuel 20:30-34 KJV}.

You must not gain everything now. Look beyond the

immediate. If immediate gratification becomes your only intoxication, your future will be empty. The ability to act on revelation is a necessity. Revelation without action is superstition. Refusal to act on a revelation makes it a mere superstition.

(ii)   Enforcement

When the LORD turned again the captivity of Zion, we were like them that dream. Then was our mouth filled with laughter, and our tongue with singing: then said they among the heathen, The LORD hath done great things for them. The LORD hath done great things for us; whereof we are glad. Turn again our captivity, O LORD, as the streams in the south. They that sow in tears shall reap in joy. He that goeth forth and weepeth, bearing precious seed, shall doubtless come again with rejoicing, bringing his sheaves with him. {Psalm 126:1-6 KJV}.

Before anybody can enjoy a new dimension or change of life, there must be an enforcement of decision. Decision or choices alone don't improve the life of anyone, enforcement does. Several people are where they are today even after making novel decisions without commensurate enforcement. David followed up the decision to favour the household of Saul for Jonathan's sake. The reply of Ziba to David was enough to reverse the steps he already took. David went ahead to ask that Mephibosheth be fetched from Lodebar. Once you are sure a decision is right, pursue and ensure its enforcement. Words are spirit; any plan you don't pursue to logical conclusion will be taken up by someone else somewhere. It is not enough to plan and dream of new dimension; it is good you see them through. Early satisfaction of the planning stage is tantamount to failure all the same. You can't jettison the enforcement of your life changing dreams.

(iii)   Information

And he trembling and astonished said, Lord, what wilt thou have me to do? And the Lord said unto him, Arise, and go into the city, and it shall be told thee what thou must do. {Acts 9:6 KJV}

The transformation experience of Paul the Apostle was made possible because he acted on the information given him. Information is key to experiencing a new dimension in life and destiny. Your degree of freedom is directly proportional to the amount of information you are exposed to. You can't experience a new dimension when access to vital information is limited. You talked about winning the city or the continent for Christ Jesus, what information do you have about it? You can't take delivery of what you don't know. Do you want to conquer Europe? Study and master the continent. Possession begins with information. God informed the Israelites about the land of Canaan before telling them to step out of Egypt.

And the LORD said unto Moses, Depart, and go up hence, thou and the people which thou hast brought up out of the land of Egypt, unto the land which I sware unto Abraham, to Isaac, and to Jacob, saying, Unto thy seed will I give it: And I will send an angel before thee; and I will drive out the Canaanite, the

*Amorite, and the Hittite, and the Perizzite, the
Hivite, and the Jebusite:* {Exodus 33:1-2 KJV

2.

God is a Spirit: and they that worship him must worship him in spirit and in truth. {John 4:24 KJV}

It is the spirit that quickeneth; the flesh profiteth nothing: the words that I speak unto you, they are spirit, and they are life. {John 6:63 KJV}

Whatever appears mysterious in your life has spiritual connotation. Whatever you can't curtail in the spiritual realm you can't control in the physical. You need to address issues in the spiritual before you can tame them in the natural world. Acceleration is not possible except it is first initiated in the realm of the spirit. If you want to translate to a new dimension, you must settle it in the world of the spirit. It will be fruitless expecting a manifestation of matters that have not been tabled in the spirit realm. Before the King calls for you, you should draw the King's attention to your plight on your knees. Events don't happen on their own accord, they are directed and controlled.

Another parable put he forth unto them, saying, The kingdom of heaven is likened unto a man which sowed good seed in his field: But while men slept, his enemy came and sowed tares among the wheat, and went his way. But when the blade was sprung up, and brought forth fruit, then appeared the tares also. So the servants of the householder came and said unto him, Sir, didst not thou sow good seed in thy field? from whence then hath it tares? He said unto them, An enemy hath done this. The servants said unto him, Wilt thou then that we go and gather them up? But he said, Nay; lest while ye gather up the tares, ye root up also the wheat with them. Let both grow together until the harvest: and in the time of harvest I will say to the reapers, Gather ye together first the tares, and bind them in bundles to burn them: but gather the wheat into my barn. {Matthew 13:24-30 KJV}

If you don't arrest the issue in the secret, you can't control it in the public. It takes spirituality to live a fulfilled life. The planting of the tares could not be executed until men slept. Your spiritual docility will permit the enemy to take advantage of your expectations. The growth and wellbeing of your wheat must be spiritually tailored in the direction you want them to go. If you must maintain spiritual balance, you must align properly. Wrong personality can make you drift negatively. Jonathan and David were best of friends, though David and Saul were sworn enemies.

And Saul spake to Jonathan his son, and to all his servants, that they should kill David. But Jonathan Saul's son delighted much in David: and Jonathan told David, saying, Saul my father seeketh to kill thee: now therefore, I pray thee, take heed to thyself until the morning, and abide in a secret place, and hide thyself: {1 Samuel 19:1-2 KJV}

Ziba confiscated the entire inheritance of Mephibosheth and grounded him in Lodebar successfully. Ziba went ahead to play a smart one even after King David remembered Saul's family for Jonathan's sake. Although, he agreed that Mephibosheth was alive, he however added a condition: he is lame on his feet. Ziba understood how spiritual laws work, so he reminded King David of I Samuel 5:8. This was a clear fight of the titans, howbeit, in the spirit.

You will recall a similar thing happened in John 8:3-11, when the scribes and the Pharisees took advantage of the law to tempt Christ Jesus. The demand of the law in Leviticus 20:10 and Deuteronomy 22:22 are that both the adulterer and the adulteress should be put to death. And the first to cast a stone must be guiltless, hence, their resort to Christ Jesus. Apart from wanting to know if Christ Jesus will fall into the pit hole of casting the first stone, they equally presented only the adulteress without the adulterer. Their motive was destructive and ungodly, so, Christ Jesus disappointed their intentions.

If a man be found lying with a woman married to an husband, then they shall both of them die, both the man that lay with the woman, and the woman: so shalt thou put away evil from Israel {**Deut. 22:22 KJV**}

King David ignored the third voice projected by Ziba and went ahead to invite Mephibosheth. If the spiritual is in your favour, no voice can barricade you. Your hatred for anyone does not stop God from blessing them. I have always hilariously told my congregants that God is not from anyone's particular village. So, no one can customize God, His blessings or control Him. People's lifting is not tied to your emotions. God does not check your anger against anyone before He blesses them. Your anger or emotions does not diminish the blessing of the hated.

God does not subject His decisions to the vote of men. God's blessings and liftings are not subject to man's manipulative antics.

A good man out of the good treasure of the heart bringeth forth good things: and an evil man out of the evil treasure bringeth forth evil things. {Matthew 12:35 KJV}

But the anointing which ye have received of him abideth in you, and ye need not that any man teach you: but as the same anointing teacheth you of all things, and is truth, and is no lie, and even as it hath taught you, ye shall abide in him. {1 John 2:27 KJV}.

When God smiles at you, no mortal can frown at you. Ziba thought he could succeed over Mephibosheth, the same manner he was successfully dropped from the back. He supposedly fell from the back without any intervention. He was dropped in Lodebar without any objection, but this time the King, David, countered Ziba. No matter where life has dropped you, God can pick you. Whatever could not kill you cannot stop you. If they could not kill you by trials, they can't prevail over you equally. Redemption laws enforce exception laws. Even in the implementations of obnoxious rules and laws, there are exceptions.

Meekness, temperance: against such there is no law. And they that are Christ's have crucified the flesh with the affections and lusts. {Galatians 5:23-24 KJV}

Whatever stopped others can't stop you. Beware of the despised fellows. They almost always emerge the game changers. Only ripe mangoes attract stones. Nobody gave David a chance when Samuel visited the house of Jesse for the famous anointing service. He understood what relegation meant. When God finally lifted him, he looked for the nobodies to elevate. Those filled with hatred at heart manifest it towards you. Like Ziba did against Mephibosheth. Don't ever be bothered. You are not the problem. They only display what they are made of. They exhibited hatred because that is who they are. We judge people from the colours of our minds. Those who condemn others reveal the elements of their minds. A wicked heart can make a saint appear as a sinner. Be careful how you run into conclusions by what people say.

Because that, when they knew God, they glorified him not as God, neither were thankful; but became vain in their imaginations, and their foolish heart was darkened. {Romans 1:21 KJV}

*It is better to trust in the L*ORD *than to put confidence in man*. {Psalm 118:8 KJV}

3.

And in every work that he began in the service of the house of God, and in the law, and in the commandments, to seek his God, he did it with all his heart, and prospered. {II Chronicles 31:21 KJV}

Therefore whosoever heareth these sayings of mine, and doeth them, I will liken him unto a wise man, which built his house upon a rock: {Matthew 7:24 KJV}

In the journey of life and destiny, your action is everything. No matter how much you pray or speak your expectations, if you don't take concerted steps nothing changes. Some people talk big but take little or no action. Your life will always move in the direction of your actions. What are you currently acting on? Even if you don't write your yearly resolutions, your actions are more important. Whatever you desire may never be your achievement, but what you work on will certainly be. Do you want to accomplish greatness? Take action. David acted on the compassion he had towards Jonathan's household. Mephibosheth could have perished in Lodebar had David not acted. Have you resolved to salvage a life? Do it now. Progress is in the doing. Although Mephibosheth had a royal seed in him, yet he was relegated to Lodebar. What is in you is stronger than what is around you. If you don't act, the deposit in you can't gain expression. It is your mentality that changes your locality. Your illumination changes your visibility. Your deposit determines your destiny. Your connection controls your collection.

If ye know these things, happy are ye if ye do them. {John 13:17 KJV}

Your condition is not your destruction if you understand your connection. Act on your connection and gain freedom. The King of kings has beckoned on you already. When you are addicted to poverty you see prosperity as impossibility. Don't suspect the clarion call from the King. Mephibosheth called himself a dead dog.

And he bowed himself, and said, What is thy servant, that thou shouldest look upon such a dead dog as I am? {II Samuel 9:8 KJV}

Inactivity is a mindset. Change your mindset; change your life. You can't encounter a transformation except your mindset changes. Don't allow bad things become normalized in your life. If you have seen too many bad things, good things may appear bad to you.

The battle of life is a battle of the mind. Your body can't act on what your mind has not concluded on. If your mind is captured your life is arrested. Same reason poverty starts from the mind. Why should you move towards change and action? You must understand that the God of heaven is the God of quality. He can only be associated with progressive turnaround. Your life represents quality. Don't go for photocopy or counterfeit of anything, wait for the original. Those who have unabated propensity for fake product also have the spirit of deception in their blood line. Don't live your life to deceive people. Don't make up who you are not.

And the three mighty men brake through the host of the Philistines, and drew water out of the well of Bethlehem, that was by the gate, and took it, and brought it to David: nevertheless he would not drink thereof, but poured it out unto the LORD. And he said, Be it far from me, O LORD, that I should do this: is not this the blood of the men that went in jeopardy of their lives? therefore he would not drink it. These things did these three mighty men. And Abishai, the brother of Joab, the son of Zeruiah, was chief among three. And he lifted up his spear against three hundred, and slew them, and had the name among three. {II Samuel 23: 16-18 KJV}

Anything you do today is preparing ground for your future. Honest steps can catapult you to the new dimension in Christ Jesus. Honest living sometimes deprives you of immediate gratification and enjoyment. Honest living can engender losses. If you want to be a beneficiary of all offers, you can't be far from compromises. Yes, you may benefit, but in the real sense you will be limited. For instance, stealing of money and giving testimony as though it's divine provision may have been normalized. Stand out. These appear as actions, but they are stand still. Don't call corruption connection when it favours you. Your goodwill today is a product of your good works yesterday. If you lack good works, you suffer for lack of goodwill. It was the good works of Jonathan that brought goodwill to the house of Saul. What have you left behind for posterity? Is it smartness in cheating people or good works towards others? Your life may appear comfortable now, but time shall tell. Saul seemed to have prevailed over David. The victim became the victor. Your offspring pay for the wickedness of your life.

Keeping mercy for thousands, forgiving iniquity and transgression and sin, and that will by no means clear the guilty; visiting the iniquity of the fathers upon the children, and upon the children's children, unto the third and to the fourth generation. {Exodus 34:7 KJV}

Be intentional with doing good. Nothing empowers character like consciousness of the conscience. When you are conscience conscious of being kind, you attract good people. When God blesses you, it is permanent. Can you imagine that both David and Mephibosheth's children sat at the same dining table? King David is the equivalent of the president of one of the world power nations today. He was made to seat so that his lameness will become obscure. It is not everyone sitting that has feet; it is mercy that has given us seats. Now, I am at the King's table. Take your eyes off my feet and focus on my seat. No matter what you have against me, God's judgement and justice has given me the royal seat.

Therefore being justified by faith, we have peace with God through our Lord Jesus Christ: {Romans 5:1 KJV}

God knows I have no feet, yet He offered me a seat at the royal dining room. If we often focus on the action we dissipate on people's lives in advancing our lives, greatness will be simplified. In God's records the feet is not the issue, access and availability of mercy is. Not every blessed man is educated. He qualified the chosen and dignified the qualified. Do you know what? Not every pretty girl is married. Those "smart" ones who are careless about God or man receive the repercussion eventually.

But he that doeth wrong shall receive for the wrong which he hath done: and there is no respect of persons. {Colossians 3:25 KJV}

4.

A nd the LORD said unto Joshua, See, I have given into thine hand Jericho, and the king thereof, and the mighty men of valour. And ye shall compass the city, all ye men of war, and go round about the city once. Thus shalt thou do six days. And seven priests shall bear before the ark seven trumpets of rams' horns: and the seventh day ye shall compass the city seven times, and the priests shall blow with the trumpets. And it came to pass, when Joshua had spoken unto the people, that the seven priests bearing the seven trumpets of rams' horns passed on before the LORD, and blew with the *trumpets: and the ark of the covenant of the LORD followed them. And the armed men went before the priests that blew with the trumpets, and the rereward came after the ark, the priests going on, and blowing with the trumpets. And Joshua had commanded the people, saying, Ye shall not shout, nor make any noise with your voice, neither shall any word proceed out of your mouth, until the day I bid you shout; then shall ye shout. So the ark of the LORD compassed the city, going about it once: and they came into the camp, and lodged in the camp. And Joshua rose early in the morning, and the priests took up the ark of the LORD. And seven priests bearing seven trumpets of rams' horns before the ark of the LORD went on continually, and blew with the trumpets: and the armed men went before them; but the rereward came after the ark of the LORD, the priests going on, and blowing with the trumpets. And the second day they compassed the city once, and returned into the camp: so they did six days. {Joshua 6:2-4, 8-14 KJV}*

The strongest encouragement is the one you offer yourself. Your giving up is equivalent to messing up. The condition of Israel did not appear to abate as they marched round the wall of Jericho; the conclusion was victory. Israel would have made the most grievous mistake of their lives had they given up. The wall remained unmovable while the march past persisted. Whatever the condition that appears insurmountable around you, will give way if you persist. The standing mountain should not dictate your response. Your expectation should be your focus, not the mountain. It is better to go round than to stay stagnant. Believers don't regret they learn lessons. When you stay too long on a spot, you look like the spot. Don't take up the identity of your problem, move forward. Several people wish they can undermine their conditions and become focused. There are steps to achieving these milestones that may look huge. In the next few pages, we shall be dissecting these steps.

(a)   Tolerate discomfort with a smile

It is near impossible to live in this world without one

form of discomfort or the other. Don't ever allow your emotions dictate your speed.

The light of the eyes rejoiceth the heart: and a good report maketh the bones fat. {**Proverbs 15:30 KJV**}

If you refuse to pray because of how you feel, you lose direction. Each time you feel funny, you go closer to the solution. How should you respond? Smile and move on. You feel discomfort because you are out of the comfort zone. There are no results and progress in the comfort zone of life. The evidence that you are on your way to success is the discomfort you feel. Tolerate it with a deep smile. Your smile revitalizes your inner strength and triggers the victory message in your brain. A little discomfort can go a long way to help you learn, grow and change. It is a sign of advancement, not a signal of setback. Each time you overcome those feelings, you move higher on the ladder of life.

Beloved, I wish above all things that thou mayest prosper and be in health, even as thy soul prospereth. {III John 1:2 KJV}

A merry heart doeth good like a medicine: but a broken spirit drieth the bones. {Proverbs 17:22 KJV}

(b)   Visualize success

The antidote against discouragement or resentment is the focus on the ultimate goal. In Number 21:6-9, the Lord taught the Jews the strategy of focus with the bronze serpent. The solution to the present condition is putting your gaze on the ultimate goal. Also, James admonished us to put our attention on "perfect law of liberty" without distractions. The result is in the focus and consistency.

But whoso looketh into the perfect law of liberty, and continueth therein, he being not a forgetful hearer, but a doer of the work, this man shall be blessed in his deed. {James 1:25 KJV}

Visualization has great impact on your brain. How do you want to see yourself? How you intend to see yourself should inform how your attention should be directed. If you visualize your future more frequently, it keeps your mind and body motivated. Making the right decisions is a function of how motivated you are. No one can motivate you as much as you can do for yourself. The most realistic thing to do is to hire yourself as your motivational speaker. Don't allow your mind do the talking alone; talk back to your mind on the goals and the ultimate. You win when you gain control of self.

(c)   Create great will power

And we know that the Son of God is come, and hath given us an understanding, that we may know him that is true, and we are in him that is true, even in his Son Jesus Christ. This is the true God, and eternal life. {1 John 5:20 KJV}

You must be able to restrain yourself from unhealthy actions that do not lead to your progress. The easiest route to achieving this is the frequency of your actions. How much you repeat the most viable steps to move you towards your goals, the irresistible your will becomes. To fuse irreversibly to your actions, repeat them again and again.

And be not conformed to this world: but be ye transformed by the renewing of your mind, that ye may prove what is that good, and acceptable, and perfect, will of God. {Romans 12:2 KJV}

You are as committed to a goal as your daily routine. If you want to evaluate the direction your life is moving towards, check your daily routines. You will suspiciously repeat those things you often do. How did you claim to win the world for Christ Jesus and none of your daily action signal the goal? How often do you intercede for the people you claim you have been mandated to liberate? If you maintain zero commitment in this regard, your words will soon appear hurtful even to yourself.

(d)   Don't procrastinate

(For he saith, I have heard thee in a time accepted, and in the day of salvation have I succoured thee: behold, now is the accepted time; behold, now is the day of salvation.) {II Corinthians 6:2 KJV}

Again, he limiteth a certain day, saying in David, To day, after so long a time; as it is said, To day if ye will hear his voice, harden not your hearts. {Hebrews 4:7 KJV}

Discipline is often about working when you don't want to. Your greatest enemy is excuse. The strongest retardation of great destinies is excuses. If you successfully overcome excuses, you set yourself on the path of prominence. Take the step now; don't wait for the right time. Meeting your deadline now enhances your confidence and self-esteem. If you win now, you can face the next challenge adequately. If you have plans, follow them. Don't give in for distractions. The

King's business requires haste. Be someone known for not entertaining excuses. Whatever has to be done must be accomplished in the present.

5

For the LORD God is a sun and shield: the LORD will give grace and glory: no good thing will he withhold from them that walk uprightly. {Psalm 84:11 KJV}

And let the beauty of the LORD our God be upon us: and establish thou the work of our hands upon us; yea, the work of our hands establish thou it. {Psalm 90:17 KJV}

It is near impossible to access the new dimension without the overflowing favour of God. Overflowing favour is divine preference for mortal acceptance and earthly selection. It is the supernatural catalyst that hastens process. If life is the reactant and new dimension becomes the product, life cannot be transferred into a new dimension except the presence of overflowing favour is brought to the reaction chambers as the catalyst. This same thing plays out in the hydrolysis of ethyl acetate to give ethanol and acetic acid which is catalyzed by H_2SO_4. Thus:

$$CH_3COO\text{-}C_2H_5 + \underset{\text{di}6H_2SO_4}{\overset{\text{Catalyst}}{}} \longrightarrow HOH + CH_3COOH$$

Ethyl acetate   Acetic acid

$+ C_2H_5OH$ platinum
ethanol

$$\text{Or } H_2 + O_2 \longrightarrow H_2O$$

$$\text{Life} + \text{situations} \xrightarrow{\text{Favour}} \text{New Dimension}$$

Therefore, overflowing favour is a catalyzer that hastens process. In case, you don't understand all of the chemical equations, just know that favour is the baptism of beautiful regard and positive consideration. It can also be seen as the acceptability without measure and likability without pressure. When people open the doors of their hearts to you, you access overflowing favour. You then command good will and unlimited kindness.

The fear of man bringeth a snare: but whoso putteth his trust in the LORD shall be safe. Many seek the ruler's favour; but every man's judgment cometh from the LORD. {Proverbs 29:25-26 KJV}

Overflowing favour is actually when the celestial swallows the terrestiality thereby making you a celebrity. Humanity enjoys the kindness of God through the vehicle of friendship. There is a supernatural favouritism and unquestionable acceptability from obscurity. No matter how Mephibosheth was hidden and obscure, when overflowing favour visited, the process was relegated and circumvented. So, relegating regulations by circumventing processes and by-passing the organogram for the lifting by mortality. There are two basic forms of overflowing favour. They are (i) favour with God and (ii) favour with man.

(i)   Favour with God

And Jesus increased in wisdom and stature, and in favour with God and man. {Luke 2:52 KJV}

Overflowing favour with God is the basic foundation that triggers all other forms of favour. You can't experience favour with man except you have received favour from God. What then is favour from God? Let us give some instances that will elevate its understanding. Have you seen people who escaped a dangerous and fatal accident yet financially broke? God showed them favour by extricating them from the claws of the devil, but the favour with men is missing. People survived the pandemic and at the same time remained stranded.

And the child Samuel grew on, and was in favour both with the LORD, and also with men. {1 Samuel 2:26 KJV}

(ii)   Overflowing favour with man

We have already established that you can't experience this form of favour except God first favours you. When God wants to transform a man's story, He introduces another man into his life. When God gives a man an assignment in your life, you reign as though it is normal. When Laban found favour in the sight of Jacob, he became blessed (Genesis 30:27). In Genesis 39:23, the keeper of the prison became blessed, because he identified with Joseph. The easiest way to attract favour of men is to be friendly with blessed people. Prosperity and abundance is a man. You can't experience favour except a man of favour enters your life. Wealth is generational; you become blessed and favoured by connecting to the principalities God has raised in those areas.

Prosperity and abundance is a man.

And it came to pass from the time that he had made him overseer in his house, and over all that he had, that the LORD blessed the Egyptian's house for Joseph's sake; and the blessing of the LORD was upon all that he had in the house, and in the field. {Genesis 39:5 KJV}

When God wants to change a man's life, He introduces the elements of favour. Life is sweet when favour is present.

For thou, LORD, wilt bless the righteous; with favour wilt thou compass him as with a shield. {Psalm 5:12 KJV}

And the angel came in unto her, and said, Hail, thou that art highly favoured, the Lord is with thee: blessed art thou among women. And when she saw him, she was troubled at his saying, and cast in her mind what manner of salutation this should be. And the angel said unto her, Fear not, Mary: for thou hast found favour with God. {Luke 1:28-30 KJV}

Mary, the earthly mother of Christ Jesus, became distinguished from other virgins of her time, because

God showed her favour. Favour brings lifting. Lifting is a sudden elevation and a departure from your peers. When status changes friends change. This is normal and the obvious reality of life. People look down on you, because you are down. Even if your name is Rose, you should know that life is not rosy. Love God despite all odds. Never question God. There are some basic things you galvanize your life with and favour comes naturally. There is no doubt God gives favour. However, like I have always opined, if all responsibilities are left for God, irresponsibility is initiated. There is a way you live your life and nobody wants to favour you. Make it easy for God to recommend you for promotion. Several things we pray for could have been corrected through attitudinal change. The lifestyle of Joseph made it easy for the Egyptians to attribute the blessings to him (Genesis 39:5).

And it came to pass from the time that he had made him overseer in his house, and over all that he had, that the LORD blessed the Egyptian's house for Joseph's sake; and the blessing of the LORD was upon all that he had in the house, and in the field. {Genesis 39:5 KJV}

(a)   Realize your ego destroys

Overflowing favour is a by-product of relationship. Ego destroys relationships. You can't be egocentric and expect favours to flow in your direction. No one wants to be around someone who only cares about himself. Joseph showed concern for others. Even Jacob who was regarded as a supplanter conceded to Laban. He served for additional six years even when he was not at fault. He reached a compromise that would enable relationship and co-exist to thrive. Ego is not bad but become dangerous when used incorrectly.

Let all bitterness, and wrath, and anger, and clamour, and evil speaking, be put away from you, with all malice: And be ye kind one to another, tenderhearted, forgiving one another, even as God for Christ's sake hath forgiven you. {Ephesians 4:31-32 KJV}

It takes maturity to build relationships. You must make a deliberate decision to eliminate small talks and gossips. Nothing destroys relationships like when your mouth lacks a padlock. People who suffer from diarrhea of the mouth can't keep or maintain relationships. Mind your business and leave yourself out of the private life of your business partner. John the Baptist carelessly lost his life because he stepped outside his core mandate. God's protection is only over you when you operate around or within your calling.

But Herod the tetrarch, being reproved by him for Herodias his brother Philip's wife, and for all the evils which Herod had done, Added yet this above all, that he shut up John in prison. {Luke 3: 19-20 KJV}

(b)   Forget the past

You can hardly enjoy favour either from God or man when you live in the past. God only forgives those who forgive other. His mercies are the carrier of favour. And the mercies of God can be enjoyed by those who show others mercy. There will always be hurts. Forgive, learn lessons and move to the next chapter of life. You sleep better when you leave the past for past events. Lack of sleep cripples the body and devastates mental health irreversibly. You do yourself a lot of damage when you dwell continuously in the past.

Brethren, I count not myself to have apprehended: but this one thing I do, forgetting those things which are behind, and reaching forth unto those things which are before, {Philippians 3:13 KJV}

Learn to be open minded, you will minimize hurts by so doing. If your expectations from people are less, you readily can walk away from any disappointment. You should bear at the back of your mind that people are never the same. Respect the differences in people.

Don't expect Mr. A to accord you the same respect and regard Mr. B gives you. Accept the headaches from some relationships, but don't ever be quick to judge. You sometimes prepare to be silent than engage in a nonsense fight. Your happiness doesn't depend on people but on your inner self.

But God, who is rich in mercy, for his great love wherewith he loved us, Even when we were dead in sins, hath quickened us together with Christ, (by grace ye are saved;) And hath raised us up together, and made us sit together in heavenly places in Christ Jesus: That in the ages to come he might shew the exceeding riches of his grace in his kindness toward us through Christ Jesus. {{**Ephesians 2:4-7 KJV**}

You are helping yourself, by the refusal to dwell in the past.

(c)   Do things regardless of the reward

Being a man that is priceless has more value than when your price is known. Nobody is a fool; people meet your price and leave you in your stranded state. Building of bridges is better than immediate gratification. People favour you more when you are genuinely committed to their course. Remove self from the center of attraction. It is good to negotiate for payment for services rendered. It is better when somethings are left unnegotiated for.

But God commendeth his love toward us, in that, while we were yet sinners, Christ died for us. {Romans 5:8 KJV}

If people reward you for everything done, then you have left no payment for the future. Don't allow your future to be empty and vacant. It is difficult to work without immediate pay, but sometimes the payment accumulates in the future. Let your incentives be a better tomorrow. If you enjoy all your life today, which one will be left for your tomorrow? The wise people make preparation for their tomorrow with their lifestyles of today. Walk away from some payment. They are seeds for your next level.

Therefore if any man be in Christ, he is a new creature: old things are passed away; behold, all things are become new. {II Corinthains 5:17 KJV}

(d)   Stop living by the standard of others.

Don't give people so much power over you that their silence leaves you questioning your worth. Accord people respect; don't do extraneous things to please them. The people you make efforts to please at all cost are never satisfied with your sacrifices. The first rule of correctness is the satisfaction of yourself and His word. If you have not offended your conscience, you have not broken any law. It is extremely difficult making efforts to meet up with the standard of others. The most difficult way not to attain happiness is to try to meet the set marks of others. Be committed to the service of God and humanity; but bear at the back of your mind the insatiable nature of man. The more you try, the more loopholes they will find in your services. Some people will have to learn how to value you by losing you. They will not see the gold in you as long as you serve them. Serve people because you are convinced it is the right thing to do, not because you expect their approvals.

Can a woman forget her sucking child, that she should not have compassion on the son of her womb? yea, they may forget, yet will I not forget thee. {Isaiah 49:15 KJV}

The rule of satisfaction and motivation is simple: go where your energy is reciprocated, celebrated and appreciated. Don't focus on what you are not that you forget what you are.

*A*nd David said unto him, Fear not: for I will surely shew thee kindness for Jonathan thy father's sake, and will restore thee all the land of Saul thy father; and thou shalt eat bread at my table continually. And he bowed himself, and said, What is thy servant, that thou shouldest look upon such a dead dog as I am? Then the king called to Ziba, Saul's servant, and said unto him, I have given unto thy master's son all that pertained to Saul and to all his house. Thou therefore, and thy sons, and thy servants, shall till the land for him, and thou shalt bring in the fruits, that thy master's son may have food to eat: but Mephibosheth thy master's son shall eat bread *alway at my table. Now Ziba had fifteen sons and twenty servants.* {II Samuel 9:7-10 KJV}

It is inconceivable to expect a new dimension without a restoration. Restoration is beyond recovery. Though it includes it, much more than the previous status or possession is attained. When Joseph experienced restoration, he was not reinstated back to the house of Potiphar but became even a boss to his former master. When it is a coordinate or additive improvement, it is less than the contextual new dimension in reference here. Restoration is exponential and multiplicative. In I Samuel 30:3-20, David's restoration was exponential to say the least. Besides retrieving his wife and those of his subordinates, they took delivery of mammoth property of the enemy's camp. The net worth of David and Israel skyrocketed and snowballed after that pursuit. Restoration is an addendum of redemption. Redemption does not cleanse you and leave you in the present state, but it recovers the years and energy wasted. You can smile because life is better. Part of what is called speed and acceleration of the adherent of Christ Jesus is usually the restoration associated with redemption.

And David smote them from the twilight even unto the evening of the next day: and there escaped not a man of them, save four hundred young men, which rode upon camels, and fled. And David recovered all that the Amalekites had carried away: and David rescued his two wives. And there was nothing lacking to them, neither small nor great, neither sons nor daughters, neither spoil, nor any thing that they had taken to them: David recovered all. {I Samuel 30:17-19 KJV}

Before Mephibosheth experienced or encountered restoration, he was a suppressed dependant of Ziba after the demise of his father and grandfather. When David located him, the hand of the clock was turned around. Take a close look at the choice of words in verse 10 of II Samuel 9. In actual sense, if you analyse critically, Ziba and his household became converted to Mephibosheth's personal servants. Furthermore, his royalty was restored. He could then feast at the

King's table were his wealth cumulated. Restoration makes you forget the pains and toiling of yesterday. Nothing turns pains into gains like restoration. Restoration is a total turn around. It is not an aspect of a turn around.

For his anger endureth but a moment; in his favour is life: weeping may endure for a night, but joy cometh in the morning. **{Psalm 30:5 KJV}**

David's relegation and subjugation as an ordinary shepherd boy catapulted him into the palace. Even Jesse, his father, forgot to extend invitation to him about the epic visit of Prophet Samuel. Can you imagine my father in the Lord, Daddy G.O, Pastor E.A. Adeboye sending an invitation notice to a family in Auchi, yet the father of the concerned family forgetting to bring all his children to the occasion? It is almost an unpardonable mistake to make. Prophet Samuel was not a usual or casual visitor to households. The father of David was properly briefed of the generational impact of that visit and unfortunately left David out of it. Restoration transformed him from the forgotten to the center of attraction.

And Samuel said unto Jesse, Are here all thy children? And he said, Thereremaineth yet the youngest, and, behold, he keepeth the sheep. And Samuel said unto Jesse, Send and fetch him: for we will not sit down till he come hither. And he sent, and brought him in. Now he was ruddy, and withal of a beautiful countenance, and goodly to look to. And the LORD said, Arise, anoint him: for this is he. Then Samuel took the horn of oil, and anointed him in the midst of his brethren: and the Spirit of the LORD came upon David from that day forward. So Samuel rose up, and went to Ramah. {I Samuel 16:1-13 KJV}

Whoever has forgotten to extend invitation to you does not matter. You will become the presiding officer of the ceremony they thought you were not qualified to attend. Restoration is undoing whatever the devil has done wrongly. Your brilliance, intelligence and comportment were tempered with, restoration will re-engineer them. In Job 42:10, the devil realized he made a mistake of his life by touching Job at all. Job became better than he previously was. Before the attack, he dominated the economy of the east, after God's visit he became the world's richest fellow. Those who laughed at Job eventually celebrated with him. Let us take a close look at some of the things God restores to us.

(a)   Fruit of your labour

When the wind of restoration visits your home, you stop working like an elephant and eating like an ant. You can't spend fifteen years in a trade and not be a master of it. When Israel encountered restoration, they received arrears of their past efforts. The God of restoration visited them and they got 430 years of salaries in arrears. Redemption is not reduction. Whatever has afflicted your labour will be compelled to restore the wasted years.

And I will restore to you the years that the locust hath eaten, the cankerworm, and the caterpiller, and the palmerworm, my great army which I sent among you. And ye shall eat in plenty, and be satisfied, and

(b)   Your inheritance in Christ

Salvation opens the flood gate of the lost glory, honour and power. Your being in Christ gives you access to two unique privileges. (i) You are able to use His name without restriction. (ii) Also, you become a bonafide owner of the word of God. These two things usher you into limitless possibilities. If you are born again, your pocket is also born again. You should not struggle with lack and penury. It is an error to carry the Bible and hold sickness with other hand. You can't be sick. Activate your healing and walk away from the sickness. That sickness is not yours. Refuse it and hold onto the word of God.

He sent his word, and healed them, and delivered them from their destructions. {Psalm 107:20 KJV}

Don't permit scavengers to feast on your inheritance in Christ Jesus. If you don't stand your ground and possession, no one will. Enforce the release of your entitlements in Christ Jesus.

8

The Spirit of the Lord God is upon me; because the Lord hath anointed me to preach good tidings unto the meek; he hath sent me to bind up the brokenhearted, to proclaim liberty to the captives, and the opening of the prison to them that are bound; {Isaiah 61:1 KJV}

You might remain a victim of satanic plundering except for the steps you are willing to take. It is not sufficient to read about restoration and be consoled. This book is not a motivational write up. We sincerely want the turnaround of your entire life. In the previous chapter we closed with the subheading on: your inheritance in Christ. Possession and enjoyment of inheritance is never automatic. No matter how gigantic the wealth of your father was, if you don't enforce the will you can't possess the riches. So, in this chapter we shall be considering practical ways of enjoying our inheritance in Christ Jesus.

Because the creature itself also shall be delivered from the bondage of corruption into the glorious liberty of the children of God. {Romans 8:21 KJV}

(a)   **Possessing your possession**
Your possession remains latent and dormant until you possess them. Do you know what? This terminology crept into the scriptural lexical after the children of Israel were liberated from Egypt. You will recall that the land of Canaan where God later told them about as the land flowing with milk and honey was the same land Abraham was told to relocate

to. Their father, Abraham, was in the land until Jacob relocated with his family to Egypt because famine. In like manner, our inheritance in Christ was originally ours. Satan deceptively stripped Adam and Eve of the Garden of Eden. The Garden of Eden is the presence or atmosphere of God. Fellowship only thrives in the Garden.

As free, and not using your liberty for a cloke of maliciousness, but as the servants of God. Honour all men. Love the brotherhood. Fear God. Honour the king. {1 Peter 2: 16-17 KJV}

The return of man to the atmosphere of God possesses your possession. Except the full knowledge and the reality of this dawns on you, you can't enjoy total restoration. So, whatever benefits you lost to Satan and his cohorts are meant to be retrieved back by restoration through redemption.

An hypocrite with his mouth destroyeth his neighbour: but through knowledge shall the just be delivered. {Proverbs 11:9 KJV}

(b) Enforcement of scriptural knowledge

The only modus operandi of enforcement of scriptural tenets is prayers. Whatever you discover about you in the word of God can only be translated to reality through prayer. Prayer is an invitation to God to intervene in the affairs of mortal men. The status quo will always remain except there is a man aggressive enough to pray. Only prayers can turn the hand of the clock around. You can't just experience restoration by confession alone. The word of God from Genesis chapter 1 verse 1 to Revelation Chapter 22 verse 21 are all prayer points designed for your restoration. The implementations are dependent on your forceful enforcement by prayers.

And from the days of John the Baptist until now the kingdom of heaven suffereth violence, and the violent take it by force. {Matthew 11:12 KJV}

If you don't place demand on life things will go in the normal trajectory. Nothing changes until someone is infuriated in the spirit to cause the change. You can't have a new dimension except for the prayers you pray unrelentedly. Time does not change situations, it escalates them. Life does not get better in line with your emotional and sentimental dictates. It takes prayers to assert your rights in Christ Jesus. No oppressor will willingly let the oppressed go free. Freedom is not given, it is taken by demand.

Stand fast therefore in the liberty wherewith Christ hath made us free, and be not entangled again with the yoke of bondage. {Galatians 5:1 KJV}

(c)   The victor's psychology

When scripture said, in Isaiah 12:3, *"Therefore with joy shall ye draw water out from the wells of salvation"*, this is exactly what it meant. Your outlook is the sum total of your status. You can't claim to be a victor but express the victim mentality. There is a way a wealthy man thinks and talks.

Then he said unto them, Go your way, eat the fat, and drink the sweet, and send portions unto them for whom nothing is prepared: for this day is holy unto our LORD: neither be ye sorry; for the joy of the LORD is your strength. {Nehemiah 8:10 KJV}

You've got to learn and adapt to another style of carrying yourself. Royalty and nobility are learnt. If you don't have it, you can't express it. There is a way to smile and dance even in the face of difficulties. No driver stops before bumps and starts crying or frowning. Challenges and problems are mere bumps on your way to the new dimension. They might occur; you should cross them without any complaints. We don't complain in this kingdom we comply with the truth of the word of God.

Now unto him that is able to do exceeding abundantly above all that we ask or think, according to the power that worketh in us, {Ephesian 3:20 KJV}

The difference between a royal child and so-called ignoble child is the language the parents or ward inculcated into them. Deploy a new dimension lifestyle. Develop the habit of the man or woman who is in charge. You are not hustling to be relevant. You are a force to reckon with. Projects fail because your interests are not factored into them. Uniqueness is not an encouragement, it's what you are. Those who dare to identify with you experience transformation and generational turnaround. You are trained to reign in this kingdom.

And he shall reign over the house of Jacob for ever; and of his kingdom there shall be no end. {Luke 1:33 KJV}

For so an entrance shall be ministered unto you abundantly into the everlasting kingdom of our Lord and Saviour Jesus Christ. {II Peter 1:11 KJV}

9

*O*n *that night could not the king sleep, and he commanded to bring the book of records of the chronicles; and they were read before the king. And it was found written, that Mordecai had told of Bigthana and Teresh, two of the king's chamberlains, the keepers of the door, who sought to lay hand on the king Ahasuerus. And the king said, What honour and dignity hath been done to Mordecai for this? Then said the king's servants that ministered unto him, There is nothing done for him. And the king said,*

Who is in the court? Now Haman was come into the outward court of the king's house, to speak unto the king to hang Mordecai on the gallows that he had prepared for him. And the king's servants said unto him, Behold, Haman standeth in the court. And the king said, Let him come in. So Haman came in. And the king said unto him, What shall be done unto the man whom the king delighteth to honour? Now Haman thought in his heart, To whom would the king delight to do honour more than to myself? And Haman answered the king, For the man whom the king delighteth to honour, Let the royal apparel be brought which the king useth to wear, and the horse that the king rideth upon, and the crown royal which is set upon his head: And let this apparel and horse be delivered to the hand of one of the king's most noble princes, that they may array the man withal whom the king delighteth to honour, and bring him on horseback through the street of the city, and proclaim before him, Thus shall it be done to the man whom the king delighteth to honour. Then the king said to Haman, Make haste, and take the apparel and the horse, as thou hast said, and do even so to Mordecai the Jew, that sitteth at the king's gate: let nothing fail of all that thou hast spoken. Then took Haman the apparel and the horse, and arrayed Mordecai, and brought him on horseback through the street of the city, and proclaimed before him, Thus shall it be done unto the man whom the king delighteth to honour. {Esther 6:1-11 KJV}

The surest and fastest route to new dimension is through divine remembrance. No matter how the enemy may contend and turn your situation into a specimen, when the hand of God comes you are remembered and propelled into your new dimension. Divine remembrance is when that act of kindness you have shown to somebody without being noticed is suddenly remembered. The payday of a man is his divine remembrance. It is when your past good is exhumed and projected beyond your mistakes. There are no individuals without one mistake or the other, but divine remembrance is when your good works overshadow your mistakes. When your time of divine remembrance comes, one's shortcomings are blotted out. Divine remembrance is a garment., when you put it on even your enemies favour you against their wish and will.

When a man's ways please the LORD, he maketh even his enemies to be at peace with him. {Proverbs 16:7 KJV}

There are triggers of divine remembrance. There are steps you must necessarily take in any gathering or unit you find yourself and your divine remembrance is activated. The next logical question should be, how do I catalyze divine remembrance? So, we shall be studying some of the ways divine remembrance can be propelled.

Then they that feared the LORD spake often one to another: and the LORD hearkened, and heard it, and a book of remembrance was written before him for them that feared the LORD, and that thought upon his name. {Malachi 3:16 KJV}

(a)   Seedtime and harvest

If you analyse almost all the characters who became beneficiaries of divine remembrance in scriptures, they reaped the seed they sowed directly or through their parents. What have you made happen to anyone? You can't be a partaker of divine remembrance when even ordinary compliment is difficult for you to freely give to people. Acknowledge performers without remembering what they have equally done wrong. It is a different ball game if you are told to give holistic analysis or profile of someone. Otherwise, make positive comments for the one the individual has done well. You can't see the good in people when their achievements rattle you. Nobody is progressing at your expense. Stop being jealous of the lifting of others, if God must look in your direction. I have always said, *"A blessing or lifting of my neighbour means God is in my neigbhourhood*". Have you congratulated your neigbour who built a new house? Sow a seed into the life of your colleague who just bought a new car. Stop maligning him, with pretense that his ways are crooked. Though that may be true, but it is not the subject at the material time.

***Let us walk honestly, as in the day; not in rioting and drunkenness, not in chambering and wantonness, not in strife and envying. But put ye on the Lord Jesus Christ, and make not provision for the flesh, to fulfil the lusts thereof.* {Romans 13:13-14 KJV}**

Imagine Ziba waiting to use the lameness of Mephibosheth to block the favour of the king? Haman worked tirelessly to stop Mordecai from being recognized by the king. When someone's time comes you can't do anything to sway it negatively. Bearing this at the back of your mind makes you act better. Unnecessary rivalries constitute impediments on your wheels of progress. This strategy has never worked for anyone. Jezebel tried it against Naboth, but ultimately was the greatest loser.

And Ahab said to Elijah, Hast thou found me, O mine enemy? And he answered, I have found thee: because thou hast sold thyself to work evil in the sight of the LORD. *Behold, I will bring evil upon thee, and will take away thy posterity, and will cut off from Ahab him that pisseth against the wall, and him that is shut up and left in Israel, And will make thine house like the house of Jeroboam the son of Nebat, and like the house of Baasha the son of Ahijah, for the provocation wherewith thou hast provoked me to anger, and made Israel to sin. And of Jezebel also spake the* LORD, *saying, The dogs shall eat Jezebel by the wall of Jezreel. Him that dieth of Ahab in the city the dogs shall eat; and him that dieth in the field shall the fowls of the air eat. But there was none like unto Ahab, which did sell himself to work wickedness in the sight of the* LORD, *whom Jezebel his wife stirred up.* {I Kings 21:20-25 KJV}

(b)   Do good because it is the right thing to do

Jonathan probably least expected Mephibosheth, his seed, to become the beneficiary of the love he showed to David. He was just being himself. If you favour people because you expect reciprocity, you might be weary and disappointed. Whatever good gesture you show to others should be a lifestyle.

Cast thy bread upon the waters: for thou shalt find it after many days. Give a portion to seven, and also to eight; for thou knowest not what evil shall be upon the earth. If the clouds be full of rain, they empty themselves upon the earth: and if the tree fall toward the south, or toward the north, in the place where the tree falleth, there it shall be. He that observeth the wind shall not sow; and he that regardeth the clouds shall not reap. As thou knowest not what is the way of the spirit, nor how the bones do grow in the womb of her that is with child: even so thou knowest not the works of God who maketh all. In the morning sow thy seed, and in the evening withhold not thine hand: for thou knowest not whether shall prosper, either this or that, or whether they both shall be alike good. {Ecc. 11:1-6 KJV}

Let the act of kindness be a continuous unabated way of life. Jonathan may have shown kindness to several other people including Ziba. In life, you win some and you may lose some. Don't take decisions solely to attract the attention or recognition of one particular individual. You can develop a heart attack when he/she turns against you instead of noticing you. Can you imagine Mordecai wanting to please Haman because Haman was close to the King? Don't figure out with sensory perception the man or woman most strategically placed to help you. God can use a cleaner to change your life in an organization where you are close to the chief executive.

Let your light so shine before men, that they may see your good works, and glorify your Father which is in heaven. {Matthew 5:16 KJV}

Therefore to him that knoweth to do good, and doeth it not, to him it is sin. {James 4:17 KJV}

Don't confuse what people say with who you are. Don't adjust your actions because you want to appease certain interests. Except you are convinced it is the right thing to do in the overall good of everyone. Whether the assessment is favourable or not, you bear the consequences. Not everyone deserves to know the real you. Stop giving extraneous explanations of who you really are or not. Let them criticize who they think you are. Keep walking; don't be retarded by fear of what people will say. Whichever direction you lean towards there will always be criticism. So, do what you adjudge as good.

And let us not be weary in well doing: for in due season we shall reap, if we faint not. {{Galatians 6:9 KJV}

10

*A*nd *be not conformed to this world: but be ye transformed by the renewing of your mind, that ye may prove what is that good, and acceptable, and perfect, will of God. {Romans 12:2 KJV}*

And be renewed in the spirit of your mind; {Ephesians 4:23 KJV}

Your mind is powerful. You can achieve your greatest dream, or you can put yourself in a mental prison.

The positioning you give your mind determines the height or dimension you reach. Your mind can make you remain small and unprogressive, and it can elevate you beyond your widest dream. Don't bother about the sizes of problems. It is the binoculars of your mind that determines the view you give to problems. If you fix your mind, you can confront any problems of life. Once you fix your thoughts, problems fix themselves.

Let this mind be in you, which was also in Christ Jesus: **{Philippians 2:5 KJV}**

The next relevant question should be, how to fix the mind. You may readily know how to fix your car and the roof of your house, certainly not your mind. Let's travel together in the voyage of mind fixing.

(a)   Readers see more

The mechanics will usually put a vehicle into a pit to have proper view of the under in order to detect the fault and fix it. If you must have a wider view of your mind, you should also put it into "the pit of life." A book gives you a wider view. It makes you have an honest assessment of your state of the mind. Don't read books by checking the volumes. What you stand to gain in a book matters more than the effort it takes to study it. A book allows you access into the mind of the author.

And Moses commanded them, saying, At the end of every seven years, in the solemnity of the year of release, in the feast of tabernacles, When all Israel is come to appear before the LORD thy God in the place which he shall choose, thou shalt read this law before all Israel in their hearing. {Deuteronomy 31:10-11 KJV}

The easiest way to consult a mentor is to devour his materials. A reader travels fastest and widest than a tourist. Two set of people see broadest view of the world: the driver and the reader. It takes a reader to know the details of a city more than those who live there. The fastest way to upgrade your life is to study a new book. If you are not a reader, you are not a prayer addict. Intimacy with God is facilitated on the platform of reading. The more you study the more you lubricate the communication with divinity. You can't help religious repetition when your reading abilities are limited.

And he took the book of the covenant, and read in the audience of the people: and they said, All that the LORD hath said will we do, and be obedient. **{Exodus 24:7 KJV}**

It takes a reader to make a good lawyer. Prayer is synonymous to a lawyer presenting a case before a judge. You can't build a case when your legal jurisprudence is weak. The profession of law is on the basis of update. A young lawyer just called to bar can floor a SAN (Senior Advocate of Nigeria) if the SAN is not updated with current realities about the case.

Intimacy with God is facilitated on the platform of reading.

(b)   Creativity is the key

Your degree of predictability depends on the extent to which you put your mind to work. Creativity is the ability to bring uniqueness and novelty into any piece of work you undergo. Don't be so regular that everyone can predict what you will say at every instance.

For as many as are led by the Spirit of God, they are the sons of God. {Romans 8:14 KJV}

No one that is Holy Ghost filled and led, who is not filled with varieties of ways of doing things. As a pastor, let people come to your branch and be taken aback by what they see and hear. Just for the sake of creativity change your style. Don't be the type who is known for one particular mannerism. You need to regularly task your mind to be creative. Stimulate different options of arranging and re-arranging the sitting pattern in the service for instance. People are easily drawn to what they are not used to. People look forward to seeing newer sites and events. Even if you repeat the same song, the presentation should be different that the applause will be louder.

If thou put the brethren in remembrance of these things, thou shalt be a good minister of Jesus Christ, nourished up in the words of faith and of good doctrine, whereunto thou hast attained. {I Timothy 4:6 KJV}

Don't readily accept things as they are; question them with a view of improving on them.

(c)   Write things down

Your mind has a limited capacity on what it can retain. If you must increase your effectiveness, you should imbibe the habit of writing things down. What you write on paper is what you commit into your brain. Do you want to be better organized? Articulate your thoughts in writing.

Thus speaketh the LORD God of Israel, saying, Write thee all the words that I have spoken unto thee in a book. For, lo, the days come, saith the LORD, that I will bring again the captivity of my people Israel and

Judah, saith the LORD*: and I will cause them to return to the land that I gave to their fathers, and they shall possess it. {Jeremiah 30: 2-3 KJV}*

Your listening skills and ability are passive when you do not write down the lessons learnt. Also writing lessons acquired, afford others to learn from you. It is wasting of resources and efforts when your children struggle with the things you had problems with. If you have put some things down for them, they would have ordinarily taken off from there.

Write the things which thou hast seen, and the things which are, and the things which shall be hereafter; {Revelation 1:19 KJV}

(d)   Focus on the Result, not just activities

Every genuine committed church member is an image maker of the ministry. So, you should be concerned about the positive image of the ministry you project. Ambassadors are concerned about the image of their parent country, because they know their rating is on the basis of the solidity of the country. It is good to follow weekly and yearly church activities, above all, you must be concerned about the positive impact the ministry is making on the larger society.

And say to Archippus, Take heed to the ministry which thou hast received in the Lord, that thou fulfil it. {Colossians 4:17 KJV}

You grow better and faster when you see your individual rise and profitability in the general growth of the ministry. Therefore, you must begin from the unit or department you belong to. Your commitment to your local assembly validates your effectiveness both in private and secular lives. Nobody works in a company without a periodic appraisal. Your contribution should be benchmarked with the total performance of the organization. Are you the kind of member that brings peace to the church authority or the one people are scared of? Do you make life easy or difficult for leadership? The things of God are sacred, how you handle them will determine how God handles your matters.

But he that is spiritual judgeth all things, yet he himself is judged of no man. {I Corinthians 2:15 KJV}

Some people are spiritual dwarfs whose contributions add no value to the ministry. How can you attend a church for more than two years and your impact is not known or felt. The subterfuge of some people is the anointing oil on them. The oil stops working the day your mind stops working. Don't hide behind the anointing to perpetuate fraud and atrocities against the ministry. The same anointing that provided preservation for Gehazi everyday equally gave him leprosy. The angel of the commission that protects can also strike. Do you wonder why things are not working the way they ought to? Check your utterances in private. Gehazi lied against Elisha, because he thought the master won't know.

But Gehazi, the servant of Elisha the man of God, said, Behold, my master hath spared Naaman this Syrian, in not receiving at his hands that which he brought: but, as the LORD liveth, I will run after him, and take somewhat of him. So Gehazi followed after Naaman. And when Naaman saw him running after him, he lighted down from the chariot to meet him, and said, Is all well? And he said, All is well. My master hath sent me, saying, Behold, even now there be come to me from mount Ephraim two young men of the sons of the prophets: give them, I pray thee, a talent of silver, and two changes of garments. And Naaman said, Be content, take two talents. And he urged him, and bound two talents of silver in two bags, with two changes of garments, and laid them upon two of his servants; and they bare them before him. And when he came to the tower, he took them from their hand, and bestowed them in the house: and he let the men go, and they departed. {II Kings 5:20-24 KJV}

The anointing on the master followed Gehazi there also. The naked truth of the gospel sounds like being brain watched. No one is interested in brainwashing you but guiding you. The price of loyalty to the anointing is not cheap.

11.

ear thou not; for I am with thee: be not dismayed; for I am thy God: I will strengthen thee; yea, I will help thee; yea, I will uphold thee with the right hand of my righteousness. {Isaiah 41:10 KJV}

Take therefore no thought for the morrow: for the morrow shall take thought for the things of itself. Sufficient unto the day is the evil thereof. {Matthew 6:34 KJV}

The expectation of everyone is to grow. Unfortunately, this expectation of growth can also constitute a source of stress. Don't be so apprehensive about where you think you ought to be. Though you may not have gotten there, you certainly are not where you used to be. Your life is a work in progress. The small continuous steps you move daily amount to the big win. Keep your strength concentrated on how to actualize the small steps. A lot of the times we fail because we look forward to mighty victories ignoring the little ones, which matter the most. Do you want to arrive in your new dimension early? Watch your daily habits, not your big accomplishment.

When the scorner is punished, the simple is made wise: and when the wise is instructed, he receiveth knowledge. {Proverbs 21:11 KJV}

The weight of your efforts may appear heavy and unbearable, keep on with the process. What you must not do is to give up. Before you realize it, what seems difficult yesterday will appear non-existent today.

When what is ahead feels daunting, remember what you have already overcome. Don't measure your progress by the comments of people. They will recommend pills that they are not willing to take. Don't blame them but ignore their distractions. The only thing you have control over is yourself.

Now all these things happened unto them for examples: and they are written for our admonition, upon whom the ends of the world are come. {I Corinthians 10:11 KJV}

So, what you think and how you feel affects your outcome, not what they say. Don't give attention to voices from outside. You only need the inner voice. You need it to run faster. The external voices will breed discouragement. So, focus on you. To shape the world positively, start with yourself. Whatever can't begin within you can't be replicated outside. You are the laboratory where victories of all dimensions are fabricated. If you are well equipped, cleaner and better success will emerge. The only option before you is to emerge a winner. You are connected between your past and your present. You past must not be permitted to pull down the present. Your focus should be more in the present with little appraisal of the past. You only evaluate to learn lessons. Once lessons have been learnt regret should not be entertained.

Brethren, I count not myself to have apprehended: but this one thing I do, forgetting those things which are behind, and reaching forth unto those things which are before, {Philippians 3:13 KJV}

Be mindful of what you permit. Who you are today is the result of your previous actions. Be determined than you meant it. You can't afford to leave your family the level you met it. You must do everything to reposition things. The name and existence of David brought the family of Jesse from obscurity into prominence. You can do much more.

I can do all things through Christ which strengtheneth me. {Philippians 4:13 KJV}

www.ingramcontent.com/pod-product-compliance
Lightning Source LLC
Chambersburg PA
CBHW071348130726
47996CB00002B/854